Benny's Saturday Surprise

CREATED BY

Gertrude Chandler Warner

ILLUSTRATED BY

Kay Life

Albert Whitman & Company

Morton Grove, Illinois

You will also want to read:

Meet the Boxcar Children
A Present for Grandfather
Benny's New Friend
The Magic Show Mystery
Benny Goes into Business
Watch Runs Away
The Secret under the Tree

Library of Congress Cataloging-in-Publication Data
Warner, Gertrude Chandler, 1890-1979
Benny's Saturday surprise / created by Gertrude Chandler Warner;
illustrated by Kay Life.
p. cm. — (The adventures of Benny and Watch; #8)
Summary: Benny isn't too happy to run into his teacher during the
weekend but the encounter turns out to have happy consequences.
ISBN 0-8075-0642-7 (pbk.)
[1. Teachers — Fiction. 2. Contests — Fiction. 3. Dogs — Fiction.]
I. Life, Kay, ill. II. Title.
PZ7.W244 Bf 2001
[Fic] — dc21
00-010257

Henry

Violet

Jessie

Grandfather

Watch

Benny

The Boxcar Children

Henry, Jessie, Violet, and Benny Alden are orphans. They are supposed to live with their grandfather, but they have heard that he is mean.

So the children run away and live in an old red boxcar. They find a dog, and Benny names him Watch.

When Grandfather finds them, the children see that he is not mean at all. They happily go to live with him. And, as a surprise, Grandfather brings the boxcar along!

Benny Alden closed his math book. "I'm done!" he told Watch. "And I'm tired of homework."

Watch yawned. He never had homework.

"Tomorrow's Saturday," said
Grandfather. "You can forget
school for a little while."
"Saturday?" said Benny.
"I've been waiting for Saturday!"

The Aldens knew why. Benny wanted a basketball poster. He had seen a cool one in a store downtown.

"I have enough money now," said Benny. "I can buy my poster tomorrow."

"We'll walk downtown together," said Jessie.

Benny couldn't wait. Watch couldn't wait, either. He'd heard the word *walk!*

On Saturday morning, the children and Watch went shopping.

"Here's the poster store!" said Benny. "Oh, no!"

There was a sign by the poster he wanted. It said: "Sold out."

"What a way to start a Saturday," said Benny.

Everyone wanted to cheer him up. Violet said, "I think that new snack shop is open. We'll get you some popcorn."

"Thanks." Benny felt a little better.

Benny and Watch waited outside the shop while the others went in to buy popcorn.

Watch found a yellow ball. He pushed it to Benny so they could play fetch. "Give me the ball," said Benny.

Wait, thought Benny, we didn't bring a ball!

No—it was a grapefruit! "How did you find *this*?" he asked Watch. Benny looked around.

They were near the supermarket.
Benny saw a woman with a broken
shopping bag. What a mess!
"Is this yours, ma'am?" Benny
asked.

Then Benny saw who the woman was. It was Mrs. Sanchez—his teacher! She didn't look happy.

"Oh...hello, Benny," she said.

"Need help?" he asked.

Benny got another bag.
Together they picked up
everything. It was strange to see
his teacher outside of school. It
was strange to see what kind of
cereal she ate!
At last they were done.

"Thank you, Benny! Hope you're having fun today," she said.

Fun? Mrs. Sanchez was a pretty tough teacher! Benny didn't think she believed in fun.

But she was having fun with
Watch. She rubbed his head.
Watch liked her! He even
licked her nose!

"See you Monday!" Mrs. Sanchez said.

Watch wanted to follow Mrs. Sanchez down the street!

"Oh, Watch," said Benny. "She's a *teacher.*"

Benny walked with Watch back to the snack shop.

"Benny! Look at this!" said Henry.

A basketball poster hung behind the candy counter.

"That's the one I want! Can I get it?" asked Benny.

"Maybe—if you win the contest," said Henry. He pointed to a big jar of gumballs.

Benny giggled. "You mean I have to eat them?"

"No—guess how many there are in the jar," Henry explained.

"Counting is harder than eating," said Benny. "But I'll try!"

Benny counted all the gumballs he could see.

It took a long time. "This makes me hungry," he grumbled.

Finally Benny wrote down a number. Now, he thought, if only I could count the gumballs I *can't* see!

Suddenly, somebody opened the door to the shop. Watch ran outside!

"I'll get him," said Benny.

"Maybe he saw someone he knows," Henry said.

"Oh, no," Benny said. "He sure did."

It was Mrs. Sanchez!

"Hello again!" she said. "I'm seeing you a lot today! It's almost like school!"

That's for sure, Benny thought. But then he had an idea.

SHOP

He showed Mrs. Sanchez the gumballs. She looked at the number Benny had counted. Then she looked at the jar. "Hmm..." she said.

She wrote down another number. She said, "Here's my guess for the rest of the gumballs. Add this to your count."

Uh-oh, thought Benny. This is like homework! But he was glad to have help.

He added the numbers.

Then Benny wrote his name on the back of the paper. Mrs. Sanchez looked at his answer. She smiled. She dropped the paper in the box.

"Good luck," she said.

CONTEST
ENDS
AT
2:00 P.M.

Soon the store owner opened the jar and started counting the gumballs. Benny couldn't wait to hear how many there were.

"188!" the owner said at last.

Benny frowned. He'd guessed only 173!

"And the closest guess is...
173," the owner called.
"Wow!" Benny shouted. He'd
won!

"Thanks for your help," he told Mrs. Sanchez. He showed her his new poster.

She grinned. "That's my favorite team, too."

She likes basketball, Benny thought. Neat!

There was another prize, too—
the gumballs!

"Want some?" Benny asked Mrs.
Sanchez as they left the shop.

She laughed. "You can keep them all. Now you can check your math!" She waved goodbye.

"What did she mean?" asked Violet.

"I think I know," said Benny.
He popped one gumball into his
mouth, and then another. "One...
two...three..."